The Adventures of Tej and Jett

Book One – Embracing Differences

Written by:
Kyle Schroeder

Illustration by:
Baginda Adriansyah

Once upon a time, in a small village filled with cats and dogs, there lived a curious and adventurous cat named Tej. He loved exploring the world outside the village and learning new things, but he was known for his rude and unkind behavior toward others. He only liked others when he saw them as useful, and he had no patience for those who were different. He often made fun of their differences and was quite mean to others.

In the same village lived a dog named Jett. Jett was unlike any other dog in the village. He had short legs, a huge nose, a loud bark, and a stinky scent. Despite his differences, Jett was a kind and gentle dog who loved everyone, even Tej, who was often mean to him. Jett was often teased and called names by Tej.

Jett felt ashamed of his differences and wished he could be like the other dogs in the village. He often felt like an outcast, and it made him feel sad. He longed for the day when someone would accept him for who he was and not judge him based on his appearance.

One day, Tej set out on an adventure in the forest outside the village. He was having so much fun exploring the lush forest and its many wonders, but he didn't realize he was getting too close to a waterfall. Before he knew it, Tej had fallen into the waterfall and was swept down the river.

When he finally got out of the water, he was lost and had no idea how to get back to the village.

Meanwhile, back in the village, another dog named Nali was looking for Tej. She had heard he was missing and asked everyone if they had seen him. After realizing that no one had seen him, she decided to go to Jett's house and see if he could help find Tej.

Jett saw this as his chance to prove himself. He wanted to show Tej, the rest of the village, and himself that, despite his differences, he was still valuable and could help others. "I'll do my best to find Tej," Jett said, wagging his tail. "It's time for me to show them what I can do."

Jett set out on his journey to find Tej. He used his stench to keep the creepy bugs away and his short legs to crawl under logs and trees. His huge nose gave him an incredible sense of smell and allowed him to pick up Tej's scent.

But as he got further away from the village, Jett's sense of smell wasn't enough to find Tej. So, Jett started barking with his loud bark, hoping Tej would hear him.

"Jett! What are you doing here?" Tej asked, surprised to see him. "I came to find you, Tej," Jett said, panting from all the barking. "Thank you, Jett. I was so lost," Tej said.

The two new friends returned to the village, where Tej was greeted with surprise and joy. Nali hugged him tightly and thanked Jett for finding him. The other animals in the village were also happy to see Tej and curious about how he was found.

Tej recounted the whole story, describing how Jett used his differences to help save him. The villagers listened with interest and amazement. They couldn't believe that the same dog they had laughed at and teased was the one who had saved Tej's life.

From that day on, the villagers looked at Jett with newfound respect and admiration. They no longer saw him as a weird and stinky dog but a brave and capable hero.

Jett basked in the attention and adoration but remained humble. He was proud of what he had accomplished, but he knew that his differences made it all possible.

Tej and Jett continued exploring the world together, embracing their differences and learning new things. They became best friends and had many exciting adventures together. The End

Talking points:
1. Have you ever been picked on for your differences?
2. How did that make you feel?
3. What are some things that make you "different"?
4. Why is it important to embrace others differences?
5. What does acceptance mean to you?

Made in the USA
Las Vegas, NV
30 March 2023

69875333R00019